To my wife and my daughter—you mean the world to me. —HZ

Published by Shekinah Press

Visit our website at www.shekinah-press.com

First Edition
Printed in the United States

Publisher's Cataloging-In-Publication Data

Zabel, Herb.
  When spiders fly-- / story by Herb Zabel ; illustrations by John Cadenhead. -- 1st ed.

    p. : ill. ; cm.

  Summary: Four young spiders struggle to determine whether their own ideas or their mother's advice will result in finding the best new home.
  ISBN: 978-0-9829770-0-2

  1. Spiders--Juvenile fiction. 2. Trust--Juvenile fiction. 3. Wisdom-- Juvenile fiction. 4. Spiders--Fiction. 5. Trust--Fiction. 6. Wisdom--Fiction. I. Cadenhead, John (John Morgan), 1983- II. Title.

PZ7.Z234 Wh 2010
[E]   2010913731

ISBN 978-0-9829770-0-2

When Spiders Fly...

May Jesus be the wind in your sail

Story by Herb Zabel

Illustrations by John Cadenhead

Shekinah Press

Mother Spider sat and watched as her eggs began to move. She giggled in excitement as four little spiders climbed out of their eggs. Mother Spider helped them to their wobbly feet and lined them up so she could look at them.

"Now, what shall I name you?" asked Mother Spider to the first little spider. He looked at his siblings and proudly replied, "Call me Biggie!" Mother Spider laughed, because it was true; he was the biggest spider of the four.

The second spider looked lovingly at her mother and said, "Everything is so beautiful, and you are the most beautiful of all." Mother Spider smiled and said, "Then I will call you Wonder, so that your eyes may always be full of wonder."

When Mother Spider came to the third spider, she found him sleeping. "I suppose getting out of that egg was a lot of work," she giggled. "I will name you Nap, because it is the first thing you decided to do."

Mother Spider looked at the fourth spider. "Hmm, what will I name you?" she pondered. Just then the wind began to blow. It was time for the spiders to leave and find their own homes.

Mother Spider did not name the fourth spider; instead, she showed the little spiders how to shoot web into the air and make a sail that would carry them to their new homes. She kissed each spider and wished them luck as they all floated away.

The spiders soared high into the sky. They could see the sun and the clouds, the tall trees and the wide lakes. They barely heard their mother calling to them, "The wind will carry you home! Trust…"

When they were high above the trees, Biggie shouted, "Look over there! That looks like a great place for me to make the biggest web ever!" The fourth spider, the one without a name, told his brother to wait. "The wind will take us home. That is what Mother said."

"Sure, when spiders fly!" laughed Biggie, lowering himself to the top of a tree.

Biggie climbed down and began to spin his web. He picked two trees that were far apart and started to spin the biggest web he could. He shot web from one tree to the other, making the pattern that would catch the most food, and the pattern that would look the best. At the end of the day, Biggie sat smiling proudly in the middle of this huge web.

While Biggie was making his web, the other spiders were riding the wind. Wonder was smiling at all the beautiful sights. Suddenly, she saw something more beautiful than she had ever seen. "Look at that wonderful thing!" shouted Wonder. "This must be the place for me, because I have never seen anything as wonderful as that!"

"But Wonder, the wind is still strong; we should trust it to take us to our new home," said the spider with no name.

"HA! When spiders fly!" said Wonder, already lowering herself to the hard pavement far below.

Wonder crossed the pavement to the beautiful object she had seen. It was perfectly round and so shiny that Wonder could see her reflection. This made Wonder love the object even more. She climbed onto the shiny object and began to spin her web. When she was finished, she sat right in the middle and stared at herself, admiring her beautiful new home.

As the two brothers were carried futher by the wind, Nap began to snore. "Wake up Nap! You're missing this great ride," said the spider with no name.

Nap opened his eyes and looked around. "I'm too tired, and this is boring. See you later No Name," said Nap.

Nap lowered himself to a building close by. As he cut his sail free, he yawned and watched his brother float away. Nap looked around and saw that he was in a bell tower. "This should be a good place to catch some food," thought Nap. So he climbed up the side of the tower and began to make his web.

After a few minutes of working, he decided he was too tired and that dinner could wait until breakfast. He climbed out onto the smallest, weakest web ever made—and Nap took a nap.

Sad and alone, the spider with no name floated away from his family. Soon after, the wind stopped and the little spider was lowered to the ground.

As the sun was starting to set, the spider looked at his new home and began to spin his web.

He did not have time to make a big web. He did not have time to make a beautiful web. He did not have time to rest. Night was coming, and he wanted to be ready for any food that might be flying around. He worked hard and fast, and when the sun finally set, he sat in the middle of his new home.

As the darkness of night covered the earth, four spiders sat in the middle of their webs.

One spider was gloating, one was admiring, one was sleeping, and the other was hoping.

Morning came, and Biggie could see many large flies and gnats
his web had caught in the night. "Oh what a wonderful breakfast!"
shouted Biggie. Just then, he felt a rumbling and heard strange
noises. A large group of runners were racing through the woods,
heading right for Biggie's web.

Biggie looked around for a way to save his web, but there was nothing he could do. The runners plowed through the web, shrieking as it wrapped around them. All Biggie could do was watch sadly and wish he had not picked this spot.

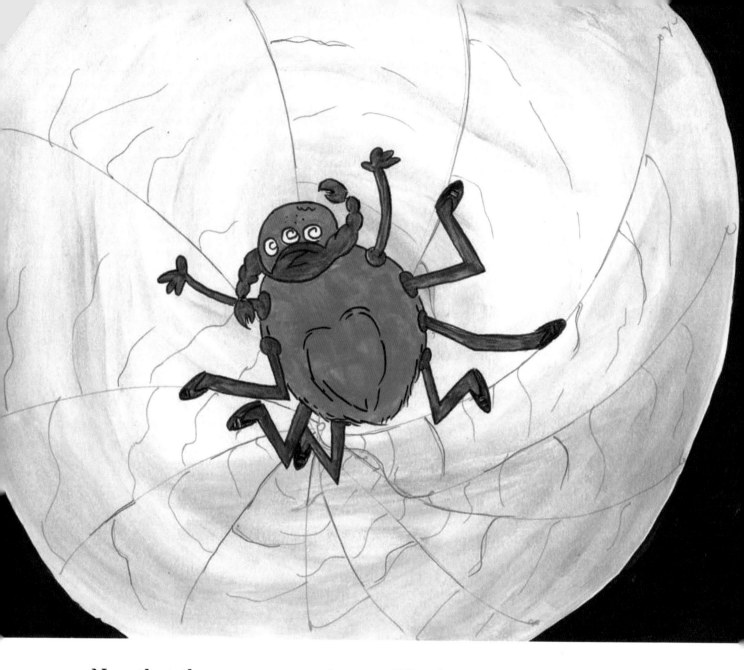

Now that the sun was coming up, Wonder could see her favorite thing—her reflection. As Wonder was making silly faces into the shiny surface, she heard a loud noise and felt her web begin to tremble. Scared of this new sound, Wonder held tightly to her web as the noise grew louder and her web began to spin.

She began turning slowly at first, but soon was spinning so fast she had to close her eyes. Wonder had spun her web on a car wheel that was now racing down the road. It didn't take long before Wonder was thrown into the air.

"This is NOT wonderful!" cried Wonder.

When the sun was a little higher in the sky, Nap started to wake up. Feeling very hungry, and still a little sleepy, Nap looked at his web. There were no flies caught in his weak, little web. As Nap turned around, he saw that his web had attracted some other attention. Nap didn't realize that last night he had made his web over a bird's nest.

Standing right in front of Nap were two large eyes, and a long
sharp beak. Nap did not have breakfast that morning; Nap WAS
breakfast.

All night long, the little spider with no name had been kept awake by the strange sounds of his new home. He was sure that he had felt a few tugs on his web during the night, and when the sun was rising, he found breakfast waiting for him. The little spider smiled big as his stomach grumbled for flies.

Looking around at his new home, the little spider noticed another spider sitting below his web. "Hello!" he called. "What are you doing down there?"

The sitting spider looked up and said, "The wind brought me here late last night. It was too dark to make a web, and I am very hungry from such a long journey."

The no-name spider saw that she was staring at one of the flies he had caught. "I have plenty," he said. "Why don't you come up here and join me?"

She climbed up the no-name spider's web and said, "Hello, my name is Grace. What's your name?"

The little spider thought very hard. "My name is Trusty," he said, as he smiled his most handsome smile. "I trusted that the wind would fly me to my home, and I am not disappointed."

Grace smiled shyly at Trusty and said, "Me neither!"

THE END

Grownups, children remember and learn well through stories; this book can become a tool for positively influencing the way they see the world. I invite you to use this book to talk to kids about the pitfalls of pride, vanity, and laziness. "When Spiders Fly..." can also be used to encourage children to listen to instructions even though they may not understand the reason for the instructions.

Here are some sample questions to get started!

Which spider made the wise choice?

Which spider would you like to be? Why?

Do you think the spiders learned something from this journey?

Have you ever made a choice that you wish you could take back?